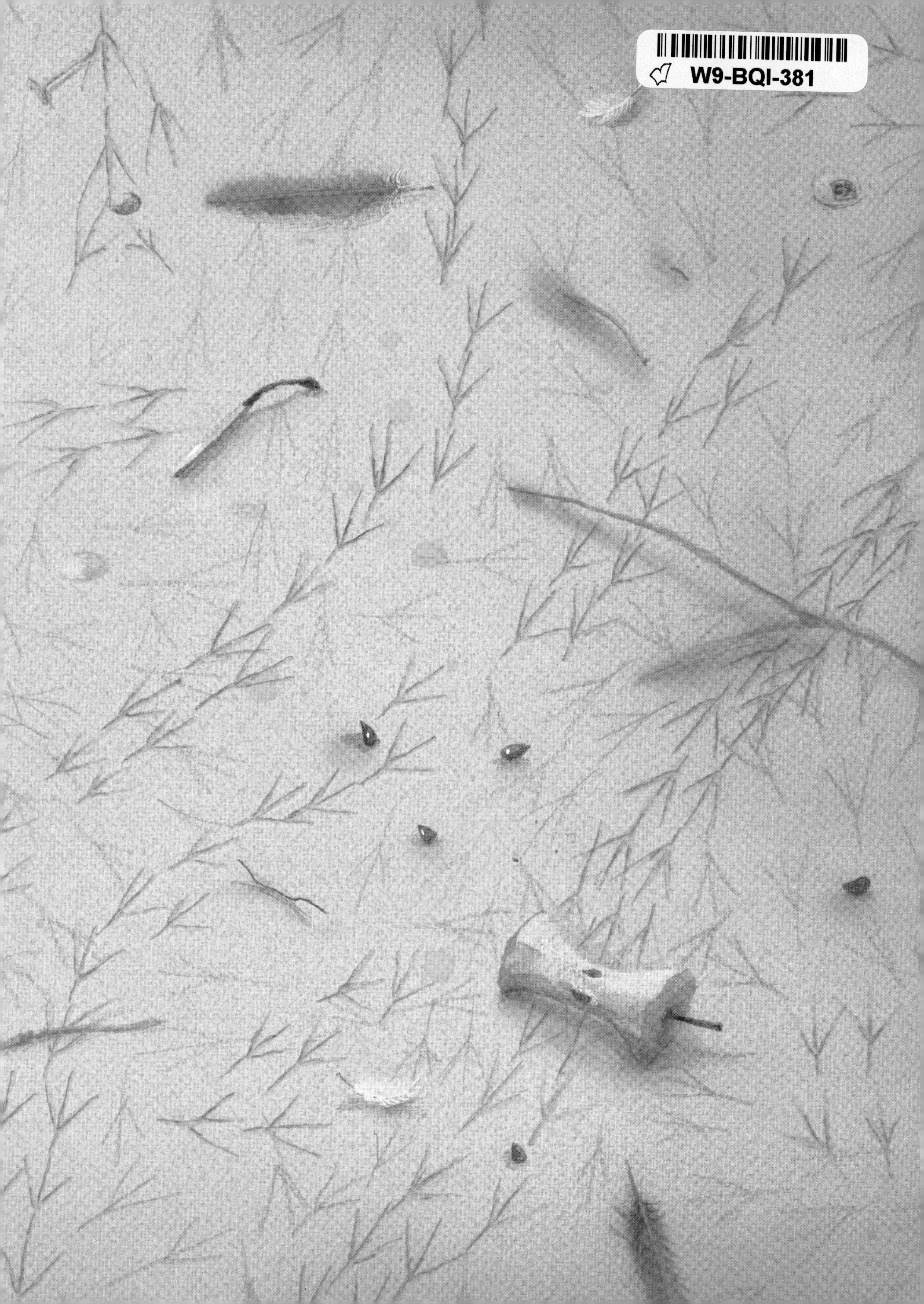

First published in Switzerland under the title *Die Räuberspatzenbande*

First published in the United States, Great Britain, Canada, Australia, and New Zealand in 2001 by North-South Books, an imprint of Nord-Süd Verlag AG, Gossau Zürich, Switzerland

Distributed in the United States by North-South Books, Inc., New York

Library of Congress Cataloging-in-Publication Data is available.
The CIP catalogue record for this book is available from The British Library.

ISBN 0-7358-1405-8 (trade binding)
10 9 8 7 6 5 4 3 2 1
ISBN 0-7358-1406-6 (library binding)
10 9 8 7 6 5 4 3 2 1
Printed in Germany

For more information about our books, and the authors and artists who create them, visit our web site: www.northsouth.com

Ben and the Buccaneers

By Udo Weigelt · Illustrated by Julia Gukova

Translated by Rosemary Lanning

NORTH-SOUTH BOOKS · NEW YORK · LONDON

The Buccaneers were a band of swashbuckling sparrows. Little Ben longed to join them, but the captain of the Buccaneers just laughed when Ben asked if he could.

"Only the strongest, bravest, and cleverest sparrows can be Buccaneers," he said. "Anyway, you're not old enough yet. You'll have to wait until you're bigger."

I *can't* wait! thought Ben. He followed the Buccaneer sparrows wherever they went, though they kept telling him to go away. Once he saw them swoop down on a café. They scooped up all the spilt sugar and cake crumbs, then zoomed away before the waiters could catch them. It was all done with such skill and daring. Ben wished he could have taken part!

Another time, Ben watched the Buccaneers tease the cat. They were flying in perfect formation. It was great! They were the best stunt flyers for miles around.

"There must be something I can do to become a Buccaneer," Ben said out loud to himself.

"I'm sure it could be arranged," purred a voice.

Ben jumped. The cat was sitting right beside him! She looked much less dangerous than usual, so Ben didn't fly away.

"What should I do?" Ben asked.

"Take a test of courage," said the cat. "When the others see how brave you are, they're sure to let you join them."

"What a great idea!" said Ben enthusiastically.

Then the cat told Ben just what he should do.

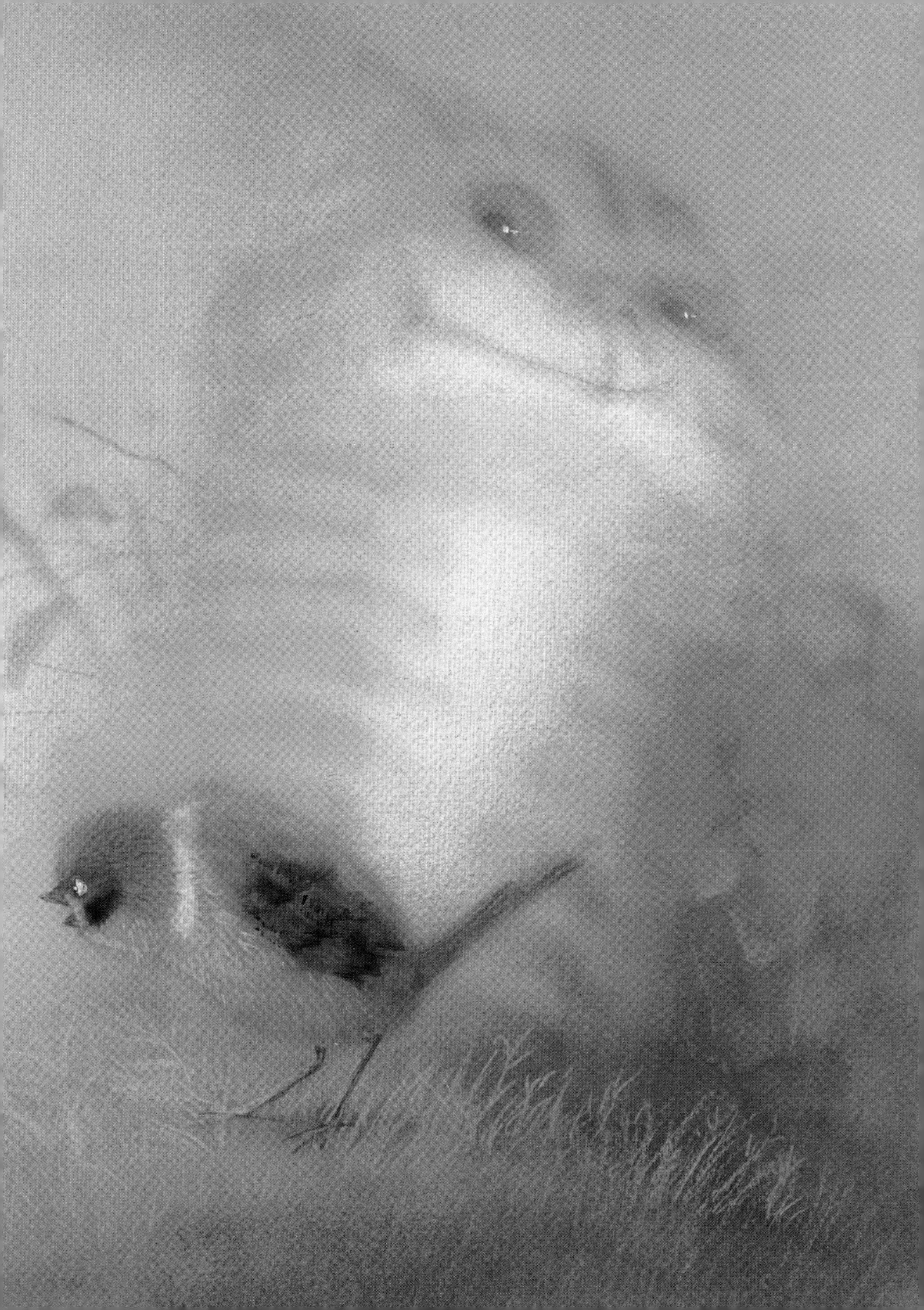

The next morning, Ben hurried over to the Buccaneers.

"The farm cat is terrified of me," he announced proudly.

"The cat? Don't make me laugh!" said the Buccaneer captain.

"It's true!" said Ben indignantly. "She's really, really scared."

"This I have to see," said the Buccaneer captain. "Come on, everyone. To the cat!"

The Buccaneers could hardly believe their eyes. Ben swooped down on the cat who cowered in a corner. Then he chased her across a field.

"Please, Ben, don't hurt me!" whimpered the cat.

"Bravo!" cheered the Buccaneers.

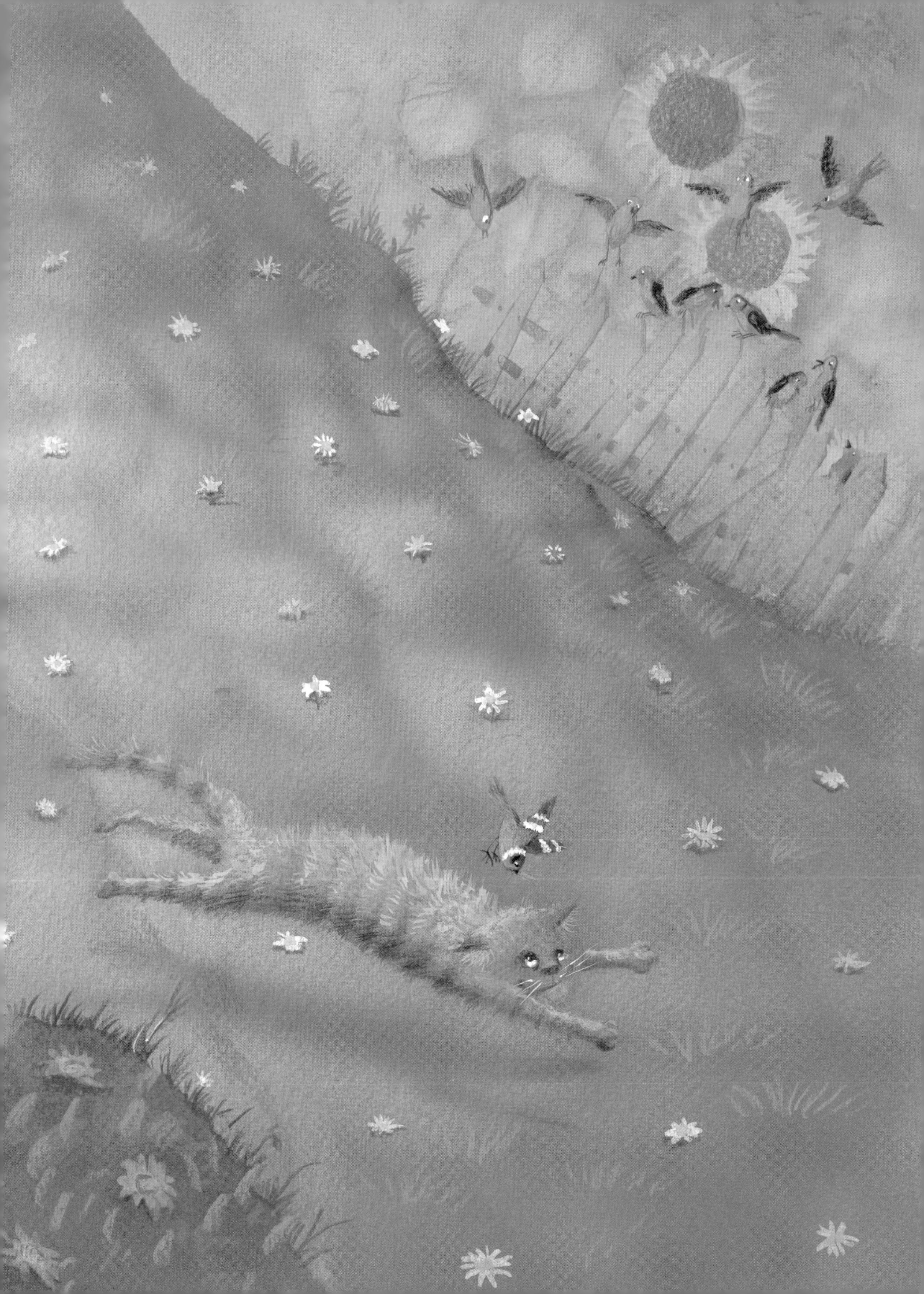

Now Ben was hopping up and down in front of the cat. He looked very fierce. The Buccaneers flew over to get a closer look. Suddenly the cat tugged a cord. The cord pulled away a stick, and a cage crashed down. All the sparrows were trapped! All except Ben, who just managed to get out of the way.

The cat licked her lips.

"Now I've got you!" she gloated. "I'll just take a little nap. When I wake up, I'm sure I'll be hungry. A sparrow will make a perfect snack. . . ."

Ben was appalled. The cat had tricked him.

"What now?" said the Buccaneer captain furiously. "Why didn't you tell the cat to let us go?"

Ben looked embarrassed. Then he told them all about the cat's plan. "She said she was trying to help me," he said sadly.

"And you believed her?" cried the captain. "Now we're all going to get eaten."

"No, you aren't," said Ben firmly. "I'll think of something." He studied the cage. It was much too heavy for the sparrows to lift.

What am I going to do? he thought in despair. Then he glanced at the cord, which was still fastened to the cage. Nearby lay the farm dog, fast asleep. Now Ben had a plan! It was risky, but he quickly seized one end of the cord and flew over to the dog. The dog snored contentedly in the noonday sun as Ben carefully knotted the cord around his collar. Ben took a deep breath, then flew onto the dog's nose and tweaked it as hard as he could.

The dog woke with a start. He leaped up, dragging the cord behind him. The cage toppled over, and the sparrows were free!

The Buccaneers flew to an aspen tree. Ben followed them. There was no chance they would let him join them now.

"If it hadn't been for Ben," said the Buccaneer captain, sounding very stern, "we would never have been in such danger. Without Ben, the cat would never have caught us."

Ben's wings drooped in shame.

"But," the captain continued, "without Ben we would never have had such an exciting adventure. Besides, he *did* manage to free us. I have decided that Ben is a true Buccaneer!"

They all cheered, and Ben puffed up his feathers with pride.

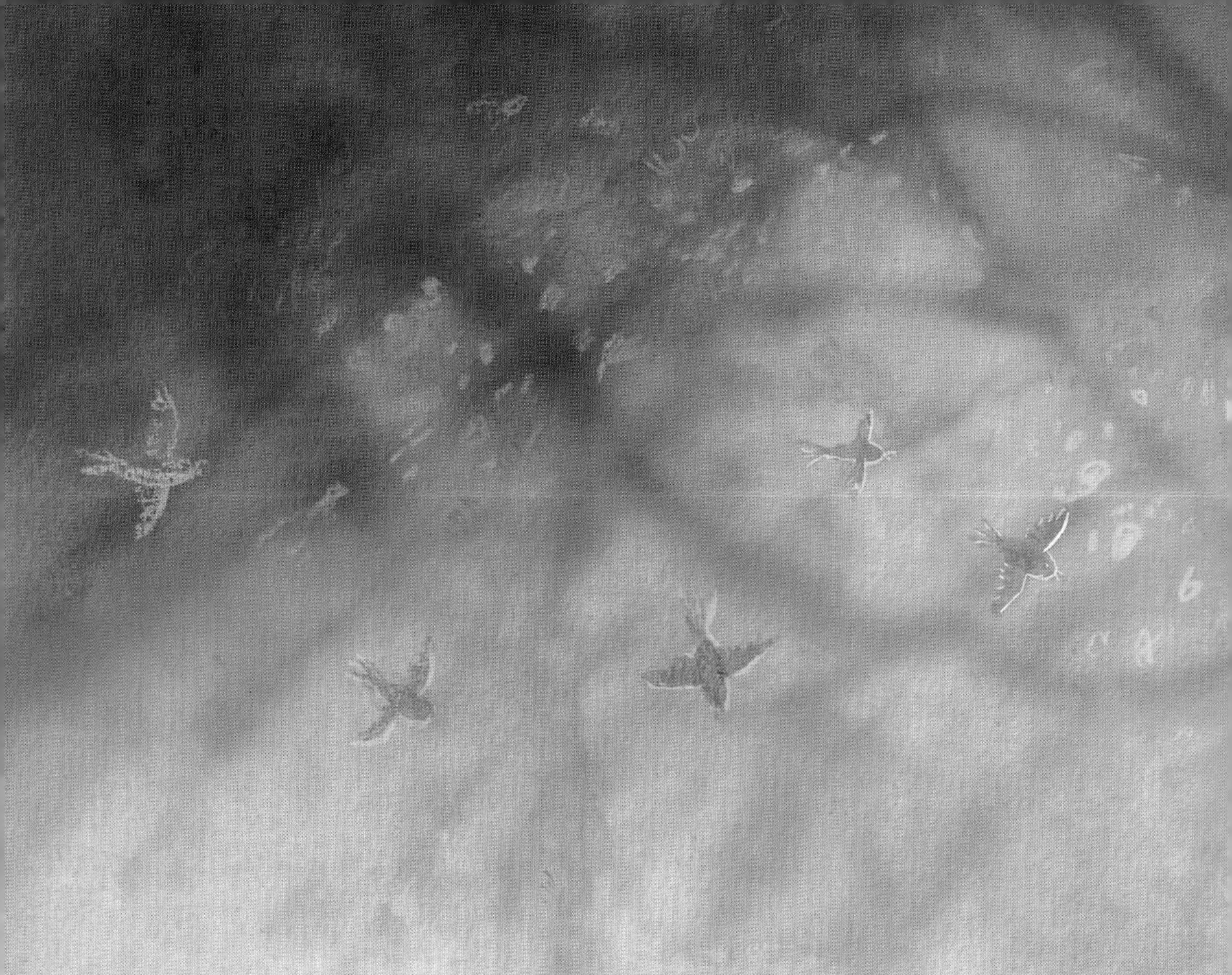

“Action stations!” commanded the captain. “We’ll raid the café and scoop up all the cake crumbs! We’ve earned them.”

Then the Buccaneer sparrows flew off in formation, with Ben right in the middle!

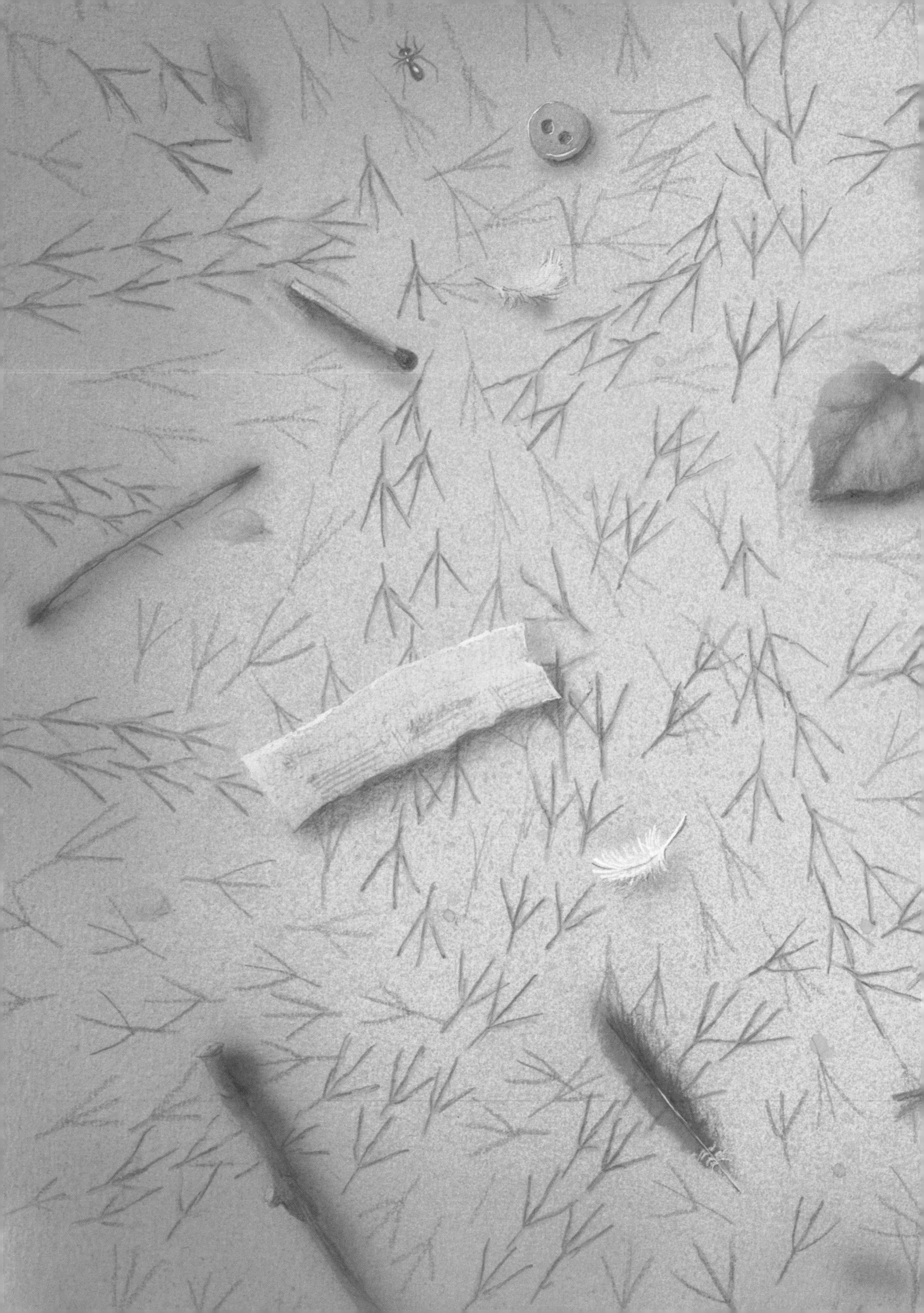